Rhio Saves The Big Day!©

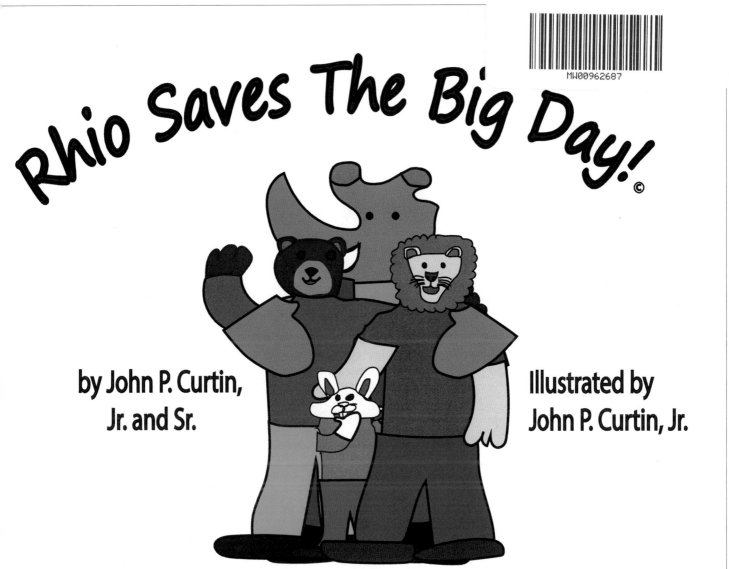

by John P. Curtin,
Jr. and Sr.

Illustrated by
John P. Curtin, Jr.

Brickyard Eagle Publishing, LLC • Litchfield

Library of Congress Catalog Card Number: 2015916470   ISBN: 9780996904407

MW00962687

Rhio was a young Rhinoceros who was always very cheerful, friendly, and eager to help everyone he met.

They always hung out and played together.

One day, Rhio and his friends were playing Basketball over Rhio's house. His parents had gone out, and they were home alone.

After a while, they all grew hungry. Rhio said, "Hey, what do you guys want to eat?" They each thought to themselves, "Hmm . . ."

They were growing impatient. Carrot said to Liam, with a worried look on his face, "Liam, stop looking at me like that!"

After a time, Rhio said, "Gather around, I have an idea. Let's have a cookout!"

Rhio brought out lots of food from the refrigerator. Then he went back inside. They could hear loud banging and clanging going on! While they were waiting, they all started to nibble at the food . . .

When the banging finally stopped, Rhio came out of the house carrying an oven. When Carrot saw Rhio he exclaimed, "We can't have a cookout with an oven Rhio!" So, he started to turn, a little sad. Joey said, "Wait!"

Rhio looked back at the table and smiled. Almost all of the food was gone. Everyone was happy and full!

Later that day, Mrs. Rhio phoned Liam's mother, her good friend. She asked her if she would bake a cake for tomorrow, because it was Rhio's Nanny's birthday. Mrs. Rhio said, "My oven is broken, and I just don't know why?" Mrs. Liam said, "Of course, I would be happy to do it."

The next day, after making a wonderful cake, Liam's mother said to Liam, "Watch this cake for me; it is for Mrs. Rhio. I have to go out for a while." Liam said, "Ok Mom."

Not long after Liam's mother left, Rhio, Joey, and Carrot stopped by to play some Football. Liam had a nice big backyard. The game was going well, when Rhio went running down the field to catch a pass. He caught it, but rammed into the house. It shook wildly!

After the game, Liam invited everyone in for a drink. When suddenly, they noticed the cake a smashed on the floor. Liam cried out, "Oh no, what happened? My Mother is going to be so mad."

Liam was very sad. He knew his mom was counting on him. Rhio thought to himself for a minute and said, "I have an idea. Let's make another cake!" "Do you think we can do it?" Liam asked. "Yes I do!" exclaimed Rhio.

Rhio got the team together, and now they were ready to make a cake, or so they thought . . .

There was flour, pots, and pans everywhere. They were nowhere near being done, when Liam's younger sister Lena walked in. She said, "Liam what is going on here?" Rhio said to Liam, "Ask Lena if she will help us." "Good idea, Rhio," said Liam.

So, Liam told Lena what had happened. "Can you help us Lena?" he asked. She said, "Ok, but you owe me Liam."

Rhio set up a plan, assigning each of them a different task. Then, they all set to work. Now they were really getting somewhere.

Mrs. Liam would be home any minute. "We need to hurry," said Joey.
A few minutes later, they were done! "Fantastic!" said Liam.

Suddenly, the phone rang. It was Liam's mother. She was nearby, but her car was stuck in the mud, and she couldn't get out. She didn't know what to do. Rhio said, "Liam, tell your mother I will help." "Me too!" said Carrot.

So, the team decided to split up.
Rhio and Carrot went to help Liam's
mother, while Joey, Liam, and Lena
stayed behind and worked on the
kitchen.

When Rhio arrived, he saw Mrs. Liam sitting in her car stuck in the mud. He waded into the muck and pushed. Carrot climbed onto the trunk. Rhio pushed again. This time the car broke free. He picked up the car and moved it to safety. "Oh Rhio, thank you so much, and you too Carrot!" she said. They both smiled.

Meanwhile, back at the house Joey, Liam, and Lena were rushing to finish cleaning when they realized they hadn't put the name on the cake. "Who is it for?" asked Lena. Liam said, "Mom said it was for Rhio's mother." So, she wrote "Mommy."

They had just finished, when Mrs. Liam, Rhio, and Carrot arrived back at the house. As soon as she walked in she knew something wasn't right.

It was Mrs. Rhio. When she saw the cake she said, "Oh my, Nanny will love her birthday cake!" All their jaws dropped. Mrs. Rhio then said, "Make sure everyone comes over to our house later today for cake and ice cream."

When they were driving home Rhio's mother said to Rhio, "Mrs. Liam made such a fine cake, but she misspelled Nanny. She wrote Mommy, but we can fix that." Rhio looked away with a sheepish grin. She smiled.

When they arrived, Nanny pulled them aside and said, "I love my cake, and I heard that you four boys and Lena made it. Thank you so much!" They all stood there with their mouths wide open.

At the party, everyone gathered around the table and sang Happy Birthday to Nanny. There was lots of cake and ice cream. Everyone had a great time. The Big Day was saved!

The
End

About the Authors

John P. Curtin, Jr. is the creator, illustrator, and co-author of Rhio Saves The Big Day! This is his first children's book. At publication, he is eighteen years old, a Campbell H.S. graduate, an Eagle Scout, and is currently enrolled as a freshman marketing major at Merrimack College, in North Andover, MA.

John P. Curtin, Sr. is a co-author of Rhio Saves The Big Day! This is also his first children's book. He is an accountant, lawyer, and former reservist. He holds degrees from Boston College, Rivier College, and New England School of Law. He resides in Southern New Hampshire with his wife and two sons.

50750781R00023

Made in the USA
Charleston, SC
03 January 2016